Catch the Sunlight

Marguerite Chase McCue

Illustrated by Ron Mahoney

D0294419

Rigby

Contents

Chapter One

Clark Gets
Some Surprises

Clark watched the ground and paused every so often to choose his next step. He wanted to avoid the mud puddles on the road to Mr. Kramer's ranch. He didn't want to ruin his new boots and spurs. They were his prizes for winning the American Heritage Essay Contest. The thought of winning made Clark smile. His other prize was an invitation to ride in the American Heritage Day Parade. The President of the United States was going to be the grand marshal!

Visiting Mr. Kramer's ranch was a treat for Clark. He couldn't wait to see Rosebud, a calf he'd grown especially fond of. Clark had been to visit Rosebud almost every week since she was born. He didn't have a pet dog or cat, but Clark liked to think of Rosebud as his own.

As he was about to step over a puddle, Clark paused when a lady's voice called out, "Please help me, young sir."

He jerked his head up and looked around.

"Who's that?" he asked.

"I'm over here," the lady's voice answered.

Clark's mouth dropped open, and his long face grew longer. Suddenly parades and presidents slipped from his mind.

His voice was only a whisper as he stared at a horse in the corral. "You're talking!" Clark said in amazement.

"I'm so glad you understand me," the horse said. "I'm Jamilla."

"I know your name," Clark said, as he hurried toward her. "I've seen you before, but I've never heard you talk!"

"I've never needed to talk to you before," Jamilla said.

"How can you do that?" Clark asked.

"You'd be surprised at what I can do," Jamilla answered. "Anyway, look what *you've* done."

Mud oozed around Clark's new boots and spurs.

"Oh no!" Clark wailed.

"They'll clean up nicely," Jamilla said, clomping up to the splintery corral fence. "But listen, we don't have much time, and something awful is going to happen."

"I hope they're not canceling the parade," Clark said, as the dark, glossy lines of his brows drew together in worry. "I'm supposed to meet the President of the United States!"

"It's much worse than a canceled parade," the horse answered. "Carrie is being sold the day after tomorrow."

"That's Rosebud's mother!" Clark cried. "But Rosebud will stay, won't she?"

"Rosebud will stay," Jamilla said, "but how would you like to be separated from your mother forever? Worst of all, Rosebud is so upset she hasn't eaten for days."

"I didn't know that," Clark said. "I didn't come to the ranch last week because I had to accept the prizes for my essay."

"I fear Rosebud might die if she doesn't eat soon," Jamilla said.

The calf began bawling. Clark's dark curls blew in the morning breeze as he walked to the fence by the calf's pen. He bent through the rails and stroked the creature's soft nose.

"Hey, little friend," Clark said sadly, offering Rosebud a small handful of alfalfa.

Jamilla shook her body and sent a tremor over her skin. The ripple startled the troublesome flies away.

"Don't think we haven't tried feeding her already," Jamilla said. "She simply will not eat. Please talk to the rancher and ask him not to sell Rosebud's mother."

Clark paused, and then a thought came to him. "Wait a minute," Clark said. "If you can talk to me, why can't you just tell Mr. Kramer about Rosebud and Carrie?"

Jamilla smiled. "I can't talk to everyone. Only a few special people can understand me. So, will you talk to Mr. Kramer?"

"I don't think I can do that," Clark said, walking back to the horse. "Mr. Kramer never has time for me. He's such a busy man."

"People can do more than they think," Jamilla replied, "if they only tried."

The sun had moved higher in the sky, and there was a whisper of a salty breeze from the nearby ocean. Bits of sunshine sparkled on Jamilla's mane. Clark reached out and touched its silky strands.

"Your mane is awesome," Clark said, standing on the bottom rail of the fence. "I've seen you in the pastures before. You're beautiful."

"I'm a palomino," Jamilla said, proudly moving her head so the sunlight played on her tresses.

The calf bawled again and nuzzled her mother's front leg. Carrie bent her white-faced head and licked her calf's cheek.

"I wish I'd remembered to bring some muffins," Clark said. "Rosebud likes to eat them from my hand."

"Won't you please help us?" Jamilla asked.

"I want to help, but I'm pretty sure Mr. Kramer won't listen to me," Clark said. "I just came to see Rosebud and find out which horse I'll be riding tomorrow."

"The truth is, I don't have much time to find anyone else to help me," Jamilla said. "Anyway, you're a very special young man. Not ordinary at all."

"Really?" Clark asked, standing tall and straightening his shoulders.

"You won the essay contest, didn't you?" Jamilla asked, swishing her tail.

"Sure did!" Clark answered. "They printed it in the Sunday edition of the newspaper, too."

"That means you have a way with words," the palomino said. "You have one brown eye and one green, too! So I knew you were special the first time I ever saw you."

"You really think I'm special?" Clark asked, with a wide grin. "Some of the kids in my class don't think so. Sometimes kids say things about my long face. Willy said it sure was a long way from my forehead to my chin.

"You have an honest-looking face," Jamilla said, "and a lovely, gentle way with the little calf. Now, won't you just have a word with Mr. Kramer?"

Clark studied his boots and spurs. They would need to be cleaned before tomorrow. He was going to ride with Señora Lily. What a great honor that would be. Everyone would see him, even Willy.

"Maybe I can help after the parade," Clark said, picking mud off one spur.

"I'll be in the parade, too," Jamilla said. "I'm Señora Lily's horse. By the way, there's your horse over there. I overheard Mr. Kramer choose him for you."

Clark looked in the direction Jamilla had bobbed her head. He sucked in his breath and stared at a beautiful Appaloosa munching bits of hay at the far end of the paddock.

"I get to ride Whistler?" Clark exclaimed, feeling the rush of excitement spread through his body.

"Yes," Jamilla said. "He's a fine horse, isn't he?"

Clark felt a warm tingle in his heart. The parade was going to be the most wonderful day in his life. He never dreamed he'd get to ride such a marvelous horse! He couldn't wait until Willy saw him.

"Well . . . what do you say?" Jamilla coaxed. "Will you ask Mr. Kramer not to sell Carrie? The buyer will be here the day after tomorrow."

The calf bawled loudly again. Clark walked over to Rosebud and bent through the splintery rails to scratch her ears. The little creature licked Clark's hand with her warm pink tongue.

"I like the way that tickles," Clark said. "I think Rosebud really loves me."

"She is a sweetie," Jamilla said. "Imagine her starving to death because she's grieving for her mother."

Clark felt the smile on his face fade as he asked, "Do you really think Rosebud could really starve to death, then?"

Then the mother cow bawled loudly and nudged Clark's hand with her nose.

"There's your answer," Jamilla said. Then Jamilla jerked her head up and cried, "Look! Here comes Mr. Kramer!"

A dust cloud appeared on the dirt road that led from the rancher's white frame house to the barnyard. Clark heard the far-off rumble of an engine as a black pickup came into view. The calf started bawling again, and Jamilla stomped the ground. The Appaloosa stopped munching hay and whinnied with a strange whistling sound.

"Run to the road and stop Mr. Kramer!" Jamilla cried.

Clark stopped petting Rosebud and climbed out from behind the fence.

"I feel funny doing this," Clark said.

"Americans are great because they help others," Jamilla said, prancing one way and then the other in her corral.

"That's what I wrote in my essay!" Clark said, raising his thin eyebrows in surprise.

"Don't tell me you can read, too!"

"Señora Lily rode me yesterday, and I heard her talking to a friend about your essay," Jamilla replied, stomping her hooves nervously. "Señora Lily helped judge the contest, and she voted for your essay. But anyone can write such things. Only a brave person acts on such beliefs."

Clark thought about his essay. He had written about the bravery of Paul Revere riding to Lexington and Concord to warn the patriots about the coming of the British soldiers. That was a brave thing to do. Even though Paul Revere was caught by the British and put in jail, he wasn't thinking of himself. Clark felt a little ashamed. If Paul Revere could do such a brave thing, couldn't Clark do something little like try to save Carrie?

As Mr. Kramer's black pickup truck neared the corral, Jamilla began jerking her head up and down in a nervous motion. "Please stop Mr. Kramer! We're all depending on you!"

"We?" Clark asked.

"Yes! Carrie, Rosebud, me, and every animal on the ranch," Jamilla said.

Wow! Rosebud and Carrie were depending on him! He felt his face grow warm.

"What should I say?" Clark called, as he ran toward the road. "I can't just tell Mr. Kramer I've been talking with a horse who says he shouldn't sell his cow!"

"You'll think of something," Jamilla said. "Now hurry!"

The pickup truck rumbled past the corral. The driver's window was rolled down and music blared from the radio.

"Hurry, please!" Jamilla called.

The pickup was nearing some elm trees that grew at the end of the lane.

Clark felt foolish and scared. The beginning of the day had been so pleasant, but now everything was just awful. He wanted to help Carrie and Rosebud; it's just that his story was going to sound so unbelievable.

Clark stomped each foot into the earth with a loud thud as he ran. It made him feel better and knocked some mud loose from his boots.

The pickup was very near the open highway, where the mountains shot up green and jagged. The sound of the pickup's engine grew dim as it suddenly accelerated and sped down the gravel lane. Clark was running far behind it on the shoulder of the road. He waved his arms, but it was no use.

"It's too late!" Clark shouted, as he stopped to catch his breath.

He kicked the dirt with the toe of his boot and stood with his hands on his hips. Small pebbles flew off the pickup's tires as it left him behind. Clark wasn't sure if he was anxious or relieved.

Jamilla raced around the corral and leaped over the fence.

"It's *not* too late!" the palomino cried, galloping toward Clark. "Watch my mane," she called. "Watch it catch the sunlight!"

Jamilla came heaving and panting alongside Clark. He jumped out of the way as she reared back and whinnied. She shook her long golden mane. Strands of shining hair twirled around her head as though caught by the wind. Her brilliant tresses grew longer. Bits of glittering light flew from Jamilla's mane into the air.

Clark's breath came faster and his heart pounded. He stood transfixed and watched the incredible scene before him. He did not understand what was happening. He only knew it looked like millions of sparklers on the Fourth of July.

Clark reached out to touch the sparkles. He expected them to be warm; instead, they fell on his hand like cool droplets of dew. Clark smiled when they landed on his cheeks with a tingling sensation. Then the bits of glitter slowly disappeared.

Clark looked toward the road and then the corral. The animals stood like statues. The pickup, too, was at a standstill, and the last note of music from the radio continued unchanged. Even pebbles hung suspended near the pickup's tire. A fly was locked in space near Carrie's ear. Carrie was caught just as she turned to give Rosebud a lick.

The palomino stomped the ground with her hoof. She was the only thing that moved, besides Clark.

"What have you done?" he cried. "What's happening?"

"I said you'd be surprised at what I could do," Jamilla answered.

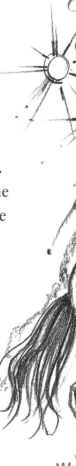

13

"I've stopped time, my dear young man. Don't dawdle—hurry now and catch up to the rancher. This only lasts a short while. Let's make the most of it."

"How'd you do it?" Clark shouted.

"Later!" Jamilla cried, racing back to the corral. "I'll explain later."

Sweat ran down from Clark's forehead, and his heart pounded as he ran past some elm trees toward the pickup. What he was doing was silly. He was about to tell the rancher he'd heard a horse talking. Now, what would Mr. Kramer say to a thing like that?

Chapter Two

Clark Tries to Help a Friend

$\mathscr{N}$othing moved as Clark hurried along in the shade of the trees. A butterfly was caught in a motionless pose just above some dandelions. The wings of a crow remained outstretched as it hung in the air near a tree branch. The pickup remained stopped on the dirt road.

Clark wanted to inspect the butterfly and crow, but he heeded Jamilla's warning. Time would not be stopped for long, so Clark ran ahead until he was several yards in front of the pickup. When he stopped running, he stood well off the main part of the road. Before he was able to catch his breath, an unexpected noise made him jump and look around.

"Caw, caw!" the crow cried as it flew into the tree branch.

The black pickup lurched forward again, and

the song from the radio blasted away. The butterfly fluttered over the fields, and pebbles flew from the tires of the pickup. Gritty dust settled in Clark's eyes and made them water. Things were back to normal.

Mr. Kramer looked surprised when he saw Clark waving his arms by the roadside.

"Stop, Mr. Kramer! Stop!" Clark shouted. The pickup drew up alongside him.

"Where in the world did you come from?" Mr. Kramer asked.

The rancher lifted his straw cowboy hat and wiped his brow. He shoved the hat back over his thick red hair and glared at Clark.

"What are you stopping me for?" Mr. Kramer continued. "Go on and have a look at that calf like you always do, but don't go bothering me. I'm a busy man."

Clark took a deep breath. This wasn't going to be easy. "I have to talk to you about your cow," he stammered.

"As far as I know, my cows don't concern you," the rancher said. "But since you stopped me and all, start talking. I don't have all day."

"You know the cow you're selling tomorrow?" Clark asked, trying to talk above the noise of the pickup's engine. "The one named Carrie?"

"Yeah? What about her?" Mr. Kramer asked.

"Well," Clark said, swallowing hard, "I've come to ask you not to sell her. She doesn't want to be separated from her calf."

"And how would you know a thing like that?" Mr. Kramer asked, tipping his head sideways and staring at Clark from head to toe.

"Jamilla told me," Clark said, wondering how his hands could feel so cold on such a warm day.

"Oh, I see. You and the horse were just passing the time of day," Mr. Kramer said, as one side of his mouth curled up into a half smile.

Clark thought Mr. Kramer had strange green eyes that frowned, even though his lips smiled.

"I know it sounds funny," Clark said, "but Jamilla's pretty worried. The little calf is so upset she won't eat. She's going to starve to death if you sell her mother."

"When she gets hungry enough, she'll eat," the rancher said, revving up the engine of the pickup.

"Jamilla says she won't," Clark shouted above the engine's whine. "She thinks the calf will die, and so does her mother, and so do I!"

"Look, son," Mr. Kramer said, resting one elbow in the open window, "I don't know why you're minding my business. I can't stop selling cows just because you like to feed them muffins. Your made-up stories are real cute, but I've got things to do in town before tomorrow. Stand aside now."

The gravel crunched under Clark's feet as he stepped back onto the shoulder of the road. Mr. Kramer put his hand back on the steering wheel and the pickup eased forward.

"But I think Rosebud really will die! I think she'll die from not eating! What if someone took you from your mother when you were just a little kid?" Clark called out after Mr. Kramer.

The pickup came to a halt. Mr. Kramer backed it up until he was alongside Clark again.

"Everyone here knows you won the essay contest," Mr. Kramer said and smiled his crooked half-smile, "but that doesn't mean you can tell me how to run my ranch."

"I'm just trying to help," Clark said, without smiling back at Mr. Kramer.

Mr. Kramer raised one eyebrow and blew air out of his pursed lips.

"The little calf needs her mother," Clark continued. "Please don't sell her mother. Please."

"I surely will," Mr. Kramer said, "but I'll tell you this. Your essay wasn't all that bad."

"Thanks," Clark said, wondering if this was

a good time to smile at Mr. Kramer.

"But you left something important out," the rancher said.

"I did?" Clark asked. He bit his lip and tried to think of what he'd left out of his essay.

"You forgot to write about how great America is because we're rich and make money," Mr. Kramer said.

"But that isn't the most important thing about America," Clark said, feeling a warm rush of anger sweep over him.

The rancher's mouth stretched into a half smile again. Clark thought Mr. Kramer's green eyes were gleaming. They were like a cat's eyes when it's caught a mouse.

"Oh no?" Mr. Kramer asked. "Bye, son," he said.

Clark started to say something, but stopped. He had been taught not to argue with adults.

"Now, don't go feeling down about it," Mr. Kramer lectured. "Don't worry, you'll learn about money."

There was a strange feeling in Clark's stomach. He wanted to tell Mr. Kramer how wrong he was about America and about money. He wanted to tell him how wonderful little

Rosebud was when she munched muffins from his hand, and how her moist lips tickled his fingers. Mr. Kramer was a busy man though, and Clark couldn't imagine him stopping to scratch Rosebud's ears or feed the calf from his hand.

"Can we talk about this before the parade?" Clark called, as the pickup moved away.

"Not likely," the rancher called. "I'll be busy getting the livestock ready for the rodeo."

The sound of the pickup's engine grew faint as it traveled out onto the highway. Soon it was out of sight.

Clark had forgotten about the rodeo that was to take place after the parade. He looked at the animals in the paddocks. Some were dozing in the morning sun, but most were awake and chewing bits of alfalfa or hay.

Rosebud had not moved an inch from her mother's side. Clark could see Jamilla pacing back and forth in the corral.

Clark wondered how he would break the bad news to Jamilla. He had tried, but he failed to change Mr. Kramer's mind. Now what would happen to Rosebud?

By the time Clark arrived at the fence where

21

Jamilla stood, he was smiling. He'd just remembered an article published along with his essay. The article gave him an idea. Perhaps he could change Mr. Kramer's mind after all. He'd have to hurry back to the ranch right after the parade, and he'd need the help of Jamilla and the other animals. His idea might work, though. It just might.

Chapter Three

Clark's New Plan

"Boy, I sure had trouble trying to talk to Mr. Kramer," Clark said. "All he thinks about is money."

"Yes, he's 'one tough customer' as the saying goes," Jamilla responded. "I presume the sale of my dear friend Carrie will take place as scheduled."

"It's supposed to," Clark said, "but I . . ."

Rosebud began mooing. Carrie was comforting the little calf by rubbing her face against the calf's cheek. Clark looked toward the cattle and scratched his head.

"You know, I think they understand what's happening," he said.

"They understand many things, and I communicate with them in my own way," Jamilla said, "but only I have the ability to speak to people."

"Why can't they talk?" Clark asked.

"Can you sing opera?" Jamilla asked, stomping the earth with her hooves as she shifted the weight of her body around.

"Nope," Clark said. "I can't even carry a tune."

"But you can write, and other people can sing," Jamilla responded. "All creatures don't have exactly the same gifts and talents."

"Do you think I should be a writer when I grow up?" Clark asked.

"Well, I'm convinced you have more than one gift," Jamilla said. "What's more, I have no doubt there are many things you could succeed at. It's your choice."

"I don't know for sure what I want to be," Clark responded. "There are lots of things I like to do."

"By the way," the palomino said, "you mustn't worry that you couldn't convince Mr. Kramer to keep Carrie. I know you did your best, and I still think you're a very special young man."

Clark's spurs jingled as he stepped on the bottom rail of the fence. He put his arm around Jamilla's long neck and nestled his head in her golden mane.

"You're my newest best friend," he whispered in her ear.

"I'm deeply honored," Jamilla said. "You were very brave out there on the road. You spoke out against what you thought wasn't right. The true American spirit is alive and well within you, my dear young man."

Clark felt a warm glow start in his heart and spread all over his body, clear to his fingertips and toes. He couldn't wait to tell Jamilla his new plan. She'd be even more proud of him.

"I'm not surprised Mr. Kramer is still going through with the sale," Jamilla said. "For one thing, he's never liked Carrie much."

"Why not?" Clark asked.

"Well, a couple of years ago all the cattle were given distemper shots. Dear Carrie is terrified of needles. When it was her turn for a shot, she ran! Mr. Kramer tried to help the vet by grabbing Carrie. She tried to get away, and in all the chaos, Mr. Kramer got kicked."

Clark didn't like shots much himself, so he had no difficulty imagining such a scene.

"Mr. Kramer didn't tell me that," Clark said.

"He limped around for days after that," Jamilla said. "Carrie was terribly sorry about the whole thing. She's always wanted to apologize. Of course, she can't talk to Mr.

Kramer, and he doesn't understand me like you do."

Clark hopped up onto the top of the fence, straddling the rails. He was anxious to tell Jamilla about the article he'd read. He was sure it was the solution to their problem.

"I could stop time when the buyer comes," Jamilla said, "but the effect lasts only a few minutes. Eventually, I'm afraid, Carrie would be sold anyway."

"I thought of a plan while walking back here," Clark said. "But I'll need you and the others to help me."

"A new plan to save Carrie?" Jamilla asked, nuzzling Clark's knee. "Do tell!"

"I read about some people who gathered in front of a factory to protest until they got higher wages," Clark said.

"That's all?" Jamilla asked. "They just gathered there?"

"Well, every time the bosses left the factory, they had to walk through the crowd and listen to what the workers said," Clark explained. "The people stopped work and protested until the bosses agreed to pay them more fairly. In America, you have that right."

"Exactly how does that apply to us?" Jamilla asked.

"Tell all the animals that after the parade we're going to gather in front of Mr. Kramer's house. When he tries to take any of them to the rodeo grounds, they should start running around the haystacks and barn. The animals should run in different directions," Clark said. Then he put his hand up to his mouth to stop laughing. "Mr. Kramer will get tired of chasing them. Maybe then he'll listen to me and forget about selling Carrie—I hope."

The animals in the paddocks began to stir when Jamilla turned to them and whinnied and snorted. Horses stomped their feet, cattle mooed, and mules hee-hawed. Chickens clucked and strutted about. Jamilla snorted and tossed her head. Geese flapped their wings and ran around the corral.

"Everyone understands and wants to help," she said. "Your plan is certainly worth a try. Didn't I tell you how special you were?"

Her words had a sobering effect on Clark. What if his plan didn't work? He stopped laughing and jumped down from the fence. He went to the cattle pen and stroked Carrie's head.

What if he just got in trouble and the rancher sold Carrie anyway? Clark realized that he'd gone from *helping* Jamilla to *taking charge* of a whole new plan of his own. His stomach suddenly felt funny. Clark stared at the green fields beyond and thought of his essay. Did he have even half the courage of the people he wrote about?

Chapter Four

Clark Gets Some Distressing News

The day of the parade had arrived, and the black-spotted Appaloosa stood near a state banner depicting a grizzly bear. There were flags from all fifty states lining the parade route in Mission Gate. Clark sat on his horse and held the reins in one hand. He was trying to make the butterflies in his stomach settle down. The President was going to arrive in Mission Gate that very morning! The Appaloosa made soft whistling sounds as Clark gently stroked his neck.

Clark remembered an article in the newspaper about the President. The story said the President loved horses and spent a lot of his free time riding them. Clark was sure the President would be impressed with both Jamilla and the Appaloosa. They were beautiful horses.

"Giddyap!" Clark said, as he and Whistler continued on down the street.

Whistler's hooves made a hollow sound on the pavement as he clattered down the avenue. The many colored flags fluttered and rippled in the breeze from the nearby ocean.

Then Clark pulled back on Whistler's reins and called, "Whoa, boy!"

The Appaloosa obeyed easily and came to a stop. Clark smiled, enjoying the pleasant coolness of the morning. He and his horse were getting along just fine.

People had already begun to place lawn chairs on the sidewalks along the main route. They wanted to have a good spot for viewing the festivities. A huge red-white-and-blue banner hung over the middle of the street, announcing the American Heritage Day Parade.

Two men dressed in blue cotton jackets passed by. They stopped to pet the Appaloosa.

"Howdy," Clark said.

"Good morning," one of the men said.

"Going to be in the parade?" Clark asked.

"Yup, we're going to be on the Transcontinental Railroad float," the other man said.

"Do you know what time the President is

going to be here?" Clark asked.

Both men smiled and one said, "No, but when he does get here, it'll be a grand entry for sure. There's nothing simple about the way he travels."

Clark could feel a tingle of excitement in his stomach.

"You can't miss the helicopters, motorcycles, and squad cars flashing their red lights," the second man said. "It's quite a sight."

"I can't wait," Clark said, letting the Appaloosa clatter on down the street.

The starting time of the parade was twelve noon. That was still almost two hours away, but the parade entrants were already arriving. It was fun watching them all try to find their places in line.

Holding the reins with one hand, Clark pushed his cowboy hat far back on his head. He looked up at the state flags flapping in the breeze, and his thoughts shifted to Carrie and Rosebud. He wondered if they were feeling scared and nervous. Clark couldn't worry too much right now. He'd get back to the ranch and help them soon enough.

A little farther down the street, two children,

along with their dog, were leaning out the back end of a covered wagon. The children waved and shouted, "California or bust!"

The sun had moved a little higher in the sky. Clark wondered if the President might be on his way. Leaning forward in his saddle, Clark peered far down the street, looking for a long black limousine—one with the seal of the President of the United States on its side.

He'll come with police cars and flashing lights, Clark remembered. The Secret Service will be all over the place. He knew from the movies that they wore little pins on the lapels of their suits and their eyes were hidden behind dark glasses. Little earphones hung in their ears so they could hear messages anytime and anyplace. Secret Service agents never smiled. Their job was way too important. Clark thought he just might be a Secret Service man himself someday, and then he could see the President whenever he wanted. Yup, Clark thought, that's what I want to be.

The shiny black limousines had not yet appeared on the street, but Jamilla had. She trotted down the avenue with her golden mane shining and her head held high. A lady with silver-white braids twisted about her head held Jamilla's reins. A black lace mantilla covered the lady's hair. A cluster of pink rosebuds was fastened behind her right ear.

Clark's Appaloosa snorted and jerked his head. Jamilla whinnied back. The leather trappings of Clark's saddle creaked as he stood up in the stirrups and waved his hat.

"Hi there!" he called, and sat back in the saddle.

That lady who's riding Jamilla must be Señora Lily, Clark thought.

The palomino came trotting up and halted. Clark leaned over and patted her side.

"I sure am glad to see you," Clark whispered in her ear.

"Beautiful day for a parade," Jamilla said.

The lady riding Jamilla had black eyes that sparkled. There was the faint scent of roses as she reined in alongside Clark.

"Excuse me," the lady said. "Have you seen Mr. Clark Lewis? I'm supposed to meet him here."

"I'm Clark Lewis," Clark said.

The lady opened her eyes wide and said, "I'm so proud to meet *the* Clark Lewis, the author of that winning essay! I'm Señora Lily."

"Thank you," Clark said, reaching out to shake her hand.

They had to squeeze their horses closer to the sidewalk so men dressed up like American soldiers in the Revolutionary War had room to march by.

"I can't wait for the parade to begin," Clark called over the stomping noise of the passing men.

"Me either," Señora Lily said. "Did you see the Pony Express riders back there? They say the President wanted to come riding in as Bill Cody himself, but they wouldn't let him. Ha, ha! I'd like to have seen that!"

"You mean you saw the President coming?" Clark asked, straightening up in his saddle.

"Goodness, no," Señora Lily said. "He won't be here until the exact second the parade starts. Security, you know." Clark smiled at Señora Lily and said, "I'm all ready to ride with the President. Look at the new spurs I won in the essay contest."

Clark pulled up one leg of his jeans to show off his prize.

Señora Lily gave such a shrill whistle that

Clark jumped. The horses' ears shot up, and they danced sideways a few steps.

"Those are some spurs!" Señora Lily cried. "And you deserve them, too, Mr. Lewis. I had no trouble putting my stamp of approval on your writing."

"Thank you for voting for me," Clark said.

"Proud to," Señora Lily said. "You should think about being a writer when you grow up."

"I do like to write," Clark said, "so maybe I *could* be a writer."

"Look here," Señora Lily said, lifting her flowing red skirt a few inches above one black boot. "You and I are cut from the same cloth."

"You're wearing spurs with your long hoop

36

skirt!" Clark said with a grin.

"I wear spurs with everything," Señora Lily said. "I wear them with pajamas, too." Señora Lily laughed heartily.

There was something wonderful and pleasing about her laughter. It was like she was telling you how much she loved the world and every creature in it.

"They're the most beautiful spurs I've ever seen," Clark exclaimed.

Señora Lily eyed her spurs lovingly and said,

"They're a family heirloom. They once belonged to a Spanish soldier who was one of my ancestors. When I was a little girl, I thought that if the stars at night made music, it would sound like the jingle of these spurs."

Clark looked at his own spurs with new interest and said, "I'm glad I'll be riding with you in the parade, Señora."

Jamilla swished her tail and nuzzled Clark's leg.

Señora Lily's eyes crinkled at the corners, and she gave Clark a big smile.

"It's the fiftieth year of the American Heritage Day Parade," she said, "and I've ridden in every single one of them. I'm a regular tradition here."

"Do you think America is just about being rich and making money?" Clark asked.

Señora Lily sucked in her breath, and her eyes grew wide.

"Why, I should say not!" she exclaimed. "What has put such an idea into your head, Mr. Lewis?"

"Well, I don't really believe it, either," Clark said, "but I know someone who said America is great because people get rich here."

"I certainly disagree with *that* attitude," Señora Lily said. "Do you know why this day is so wonderful? You see representations of all the people who made sacrifices to build a strong America."

Two horsemen came riding up to join them. One was dressed as General Lee, and the other was dressed as General Grant. Both men tipped their hats to Señora Lily before speaking.

"Good morning, Señora Lily," said 'General Lee.'

"Good morning, gentlemen!" she said, and motioned toward Clark. "This is Mr. Clark Lewis. He won the essay contest."

"Morning," said 'General Lee,' tipping his hat again.

"Fine essay," said 'General Grant.'

"This is Mr. Devroe and Mr. Shaw," Señora Lily said, pointing to each man in turn.

Mr. Devroe's horse whinnied and nudged Jamilla's side. Jamilla responded with a whinny of her own and perked up her ears. Clark wondered if they could be talking the way Jamilla said animals could talk.

"Mr. Lewis, please excuse us while we chat a moment," Señora Lily said. "These men are old friends who've just arrived for the parade."

Señora Lily turned toward the men and began chatting, her lace mantilla fluttering in the breeze. Jamilla jerked her head up and down, and began dancing in place nervously. Whistler's legs and body stiffened and he pulled at the reins. Clark patted the side of his horse to calm him.

"Steady there," Señora Lily said to Jamilla, and returned to her conversation.

"Something awful has happened," Jamilla whispered to Clark. "Mr. Devroe and Mr. Shaw have just arrived from Mr. Kramer's ranch. Mr. Devroe's horse told me the man who's buying Carrie has arrived a day early! He's there making the purchase even as we speak."

Clark's heart skipped a beat, and it seemed like the blue sky had turned gray. He lifted his hat and wiped his forehead. The sun suddenly seemed much hotter.

"That's awful!" he cried.

Señora Lily's group stopped talking and stared at Clark.

"What's wrong?" Mr. Shaw asked, giving Clark a puzzled look.

"Uh, uh . . . It's hard to explain," Clark said.

"Well, the sun is getting hotter, and the street is getting crowded. And I wish the President would hurry up and get here."

Clark knew Jamilla's talk would only sound like snorts and whinnies to anyone else but him. Yet he wondered what Señora Lily would think if she heard Jamilla actually talking.

"There is still almost an hour to go until parade time," Mr. Devroe said.

The group went back to its conversation. Some children walked by with confetti-filled eggs. They broke the eggs and took turns sprinkling confetti on each other's hair. Clark gave them only a quick glance as he whispered to Jamilla. "What'll we do now?" he asked.

"We must hurry back to the ranch and carry out your plan," Jamilla said, clomping the pavement restlessly with her hooves. "There's not a moment to lose."

"What about the President and the parade?" Clark asked, making sure he spoke in a soft voice.

"You must decide quickly!" Jamilla responded. "Will you help a friend or stay and enjoy a day of glory?"

Clark's breath came faster. He felt frustration

welling up inside him. It wasn't fair for him to have to decide such a thing. This was to be his day! He'd worked hard writing his essay and the President was coming to meet him. All his friends from school would be watching—even Willy, who teased him about his long face. Everyone would see Clark Lewis riding right behind the Commander-in-Chief. There was sure to be an article in the paper about it. Should he sacrifice everything for a plan that might not even work?

Chapter Five

Clark Makes an Important Choice

The Appaloosa was chomping at his bit. Jamilla brushed against him while she danced in place.

"Steady, girl!" Señora Lily cried, as Mr. Devroe reached out to help her calm the horse. "I can't imagine what's gotten into her," Señora Lily remarked.

Clark felt Whistler panting and straining. Jamilla stretched her long neck toward Clark and spoke with a tenseness in her voice.

"Our country's history is a never-ending story of bravery and sacrifices," Jamilla said.

Clark's heart skipped a beat. Those were his words! The very things he had written in his essay.

Señora Lily and her two friends were chatting away and seemed unaware of what was taking place between Clark and Jamilla. Every once in a while, Mr. Devroe or Mr. Shaw said something that brought out Señora Lily's wonderful laughter.

"Sacajawea will be in the parade," Mr. Shaw said. "I saw her just a minute ago."

Clark noticed a woman on a float dressed as the explorers Lewis and Clark's famous guide, Sacajawea. Clark had written about how Sacajawea bravely helped Lewis and Clark save their precious equipment from a sinking boat. He pictured her grabbing compasses and medical supplies from a boat that was quickly filling with water from an angry river.

"She didn't think about herself," Clark said to himself. "She just did what she had to do," he said a bit louder.

Señora Lily and her friends had stopped talking. They held their reins and stared at Clark. He realized he'd been talking too loudly. It seemed like Señora Lily wanted to ask him a question, but she didn't. If only she knew about Carrie and Rosebud. Clark knew that at that very minute they must be waiting for him to come save them. He was their only hope.

Jamilla pranced two steps forward to move

over for a line of antique cars passing by. She was now about as close to Clark as she could get.

She spoke quickly, "Well, what are you going to do, my dear young man?"

Before Clark could answer, Señora Lily said, "Every time I think of that young woman struggling around in that cold, swirling water to save things for the Lewis and Clark expedition, I just get goose bumps! Such an unselfish act. Clark wrote that part so well."

A funny sensation had started in Clark's stomach. It was a kind of excitement that traveled to his heart and made the roots of his hair feel tingly.

"The Pony Express riders were the same way," Mr. Devroe said. "They got the U.S. mail through, no matter what."

Clark's heart was beating wildly. Even his fingertips felt excited. There was no doubt about what his duty was that day. His mouth went dry and his hands shook.

"Yee-haw!" Clark shouted, whipping his hat from his head. He waved the hat in the air and spurred his horse.

The Appaloosa reared up, and Clark

clutched the reins, shouting, "Giddyap, Whistler!"

People on the streets stopped laughing and chatting as they stared Clark's way. Mr. Shaw and Mr. Devroe looked shocked as Clark's horse leaped forward. Clark bent low over the saddle just as he'd always pictured Paul Revere doing on the night of his famous ride. The Appaloosa seemed only too pleased to be charging forth down the street. The horse's hooves clattered on the pavement as people gawked. Clark was breathing hard, and his legs hugged his horse's sides. He used one hand to shove his hat far down on his head. He glanced backward to see what the others were doing. It was just as he thought. Jamilla and Señora Lily were galloping right behind him.

"What's gotten into you?" Mr. Shaw called.

"Come back in time for the parade lineup!" Mr. Devroe cried.

Señora Lily's mantilla flew off her head, but she held her reins and rode like the wind on Jamilla's back.

"Now this is riding!" Señora Lily cried, as her long red skirt rippled in the wind.

The riders whizzed by a red-white-and-blue

float bearing a huge replica of the Constitution of the United States. They passed a man with a bubble-making machine that sent dozens of shiny bubbles their way.

A little girl with green ribbons in her hair pointed and asked, "Is that the parade, Mommy?"

"There are too many people in the streets!" Jamilla cried, galloping up alongside Clark.

"We'll have to slow down to ride around them," Clark answered.

"There's a better way," Jamilla said, slowing to a trot.

At first Clark didn't realize what she meant and was annoyed when she came to a halt. He drew up alongside the palomino and was about to say something when he saw her mane begin to shimmer in the sunlight.

A giddy feeling of excitement shot through Clark's body. She's going to do it, he thought. Jamilla's going to stop time again!

Chapter Six

Clark Rides
to the Rescue

The brilliant sun was moving higher in the sky. Jamilla's long mane caught sparkles of light. She shook her head so the strands of her golden mane grew longer. Her shining tresses twirled about her head and spiraled into the air as though caught by the wind. A million specks of light shot from her mane. A whirlwind of shimmering light surrounded Clark. He knew how it must feel to be inside a star.

Señora Lily was smiling at him, but Clark was too caught up in the moment to speak to her. The volley of sparkles began to fade, and Clark sighed. It was over too soon. He placed his reins over the saddle horn and held out his hands to touch the last bits of light. He sat staring at his fingers for a moment before he picked up his reins.

"That was beautiful," he said.

"It always is," Señora Lily replied.

"You know about Jamilla's gift?" Clark asked. "Can you talk to her, too?"

"Of course," Señora Lily said. "She and I are old and dear friends, but I didn't know you and Jamilla were friends, too. Then I heard bits of your chatter when I was talking with Mr. Shaw and Mr. Devroe. I was surprised, but only for a second."

"Well then, why were we whispering back there before Jamilla made time stop?" Clark asked.

"We weren't all whispering," Jamilla said. "Only you were."

"Why didn't you tell me all this?" Clark asked, trying not to sound too annoyed.

"I meant to," Jamilla said, "but all this happened before I had the chance. Besides, we had to consider Señora Lily's friends and what they'd think about a boy who has conversations with a horse. Look where you're going and don't run into anyone!"

Clark rode around people who were standing like statues on the street. The little girl with the green ribbons stood still, her finger pointing to a cotton-candy machine. Wagons and buggies were at a standstill. The horses pulling them were caught with their legs raised in midstep.

Instead of fluttering about, the state flags were motionless. Bubbles from the bubble machine hung still in the air. Clark reached out to touch one, but Jamilla stopped him.

"No, no!" she said. "Touch anything and time will instantly resume."

50

"You mean we can only use this to move ourselves ahead a little bit?"

"Exactly," Jamilla answered.

Señora Lily laughed and pointed as she jogged along on Jamilla's back.

"Isn't that cute?" Señora Lily asked.

A couple of children stood with bits of confetti locked in the air above their heads.

"What's that humming sound?" Clark asked.

"That's how talk sounds if you make it come to a screeching halt," Jamilla replied.

51

A police siren's wail became one shrill, unwavering note.

"We better stop talking and get to the ranch," Jamilla said. "I hope we get there before the buyer leaves with Carrie."

The two riders had to maneuver themselves around people, floats, soldiers, covered wagons, police cars, and children.

"If Carrie is taken away from Rosebud, I fear the little calf will be so distraught that she won't eat and she may die!" Jamilla cried.

"Then let's make tracks!" Señora Lily said.

"Yee-haw!" Clark cried, giving his horse's reins a shake.

Both horses broke into an open gallop as they left Mission Gate and took the highway between the mountains and the ocean. The air felt refreshing on Clark's skin.

Clark laughed and pointed. "Look!" he said. "Have you ever seen the ocean standing still before?"

The white-capped waves were long, frozen wedges of foam. The rocking and rolling of the ocean had stopped. A seagull was fixed in the air above the water. Gone was the rhythmic sound of the ocean as it crashed against the shore.

There was only a steady monotonous hiss from a tide caught in the grip of unchanging time.

As they galloped along, Clark told Señora Lily how he'd already tried to talk to Mr. Kramer about Carrie and Rosebud. He couldn't help adding that Mr. Kramer was the one who said America was great because of money.

"Well, shame on him," Señora Lily said, as she bounced along. "As for the cow, I know how she feels. My daughter joined the Peace Corps, and I miss her so much."

"It's over!" Jamilla cried, as she lurched forward at a faster gallop.

The hissing sound was broken by a thunderous roar as ocean waves crashed against the shore once more.

"Time is moving forward again," Señora Lily cried, "so we'd better hurry."

A seagull soared overhead as the riders left the main highway and clattered down a dusty gravel road. They sped by green fields and groves of oak trees, leaving the ocean far behind them.

"I'm taking a shortcut," Jamilla announced. The palomino leaped across a ditch that was filled with sunflowers. She raced across a field and jumped over a barbed wire fence.

The Appaloosa leaped the same ditch and fence easily. Clark silently thanked his grandparents for the riding lessons they'd given him for a birthday present one year. He kept his eye on Señora Lily. They were riding hard and he was afraid she might fall, but she took the jumps with fine form.

"Be careful, Señora," Clark called, just to reassure himself.

Señora Lily laughed heartily and cried, "I'm wearing my Spanish silver spurs! I've never fallen from my horse while I had them on. I'm sure they helped me win the Mission Gate Equestrian Grand Prize."

"Do you think I'd let anything happen to Señora Lily?" Jamilla cried, with a note of exasperation in her voice. She snorted and cried, "Never!"

"Look!" Clark shouted, pointing to a pebbled lane lined with elm trees. "There's the road to Mr. Kramer's house. I hope we're not too late to save Carrie."

The rancher's white frame house was about a half a mile down the road. A wide gravel driveway circled the front of the house and led around back toward the corral and barn.

A blue cattle truck was parked in front of the house. This was the only sign of the man who'd come to buy Carrie.

The horses slowed to a trot. They were panting, their sides glossy with sweat. Clark lifted his hat and wiped the sweat away. As Señora Lily began to dismount, Clark hopped off his horse to help her.

"I'm sorry for the awful ride, Señora," he said.

"Why that was the best hoof-pounding, fence-jumping ride I've had in fifty years!" she exclaimed. "Paul Revere himself couldn't have had a better ride."

"But you've missed meeting the President," Clark said.

"So did you," Señora Lily said. "Now let's tend to business here. Someone needs our help, I understand."

There was a pang in Clark's heart as he thought of what he was missing. Someone would ride with the President today, but it wouldn't be him. Willy would probably tease him about missing the parade, and his parents would ask a hundred questions. How could he ever explain things to his family and friends?

The screen door banged open. Mr. Kramer stepped out onto the porch. A tall man wearing a wide-brimmed, white hat followed Mr. Kramer out. The man had on a western-style shirt, well-worn jeans, and black boots.

Then came a lovely sound. Clark looked at the man's feet. Silver spurs jingled on the man's boots as he walked out onto the porch.

Mr. Kramer frowned when he saw Clark.

"I thought I heard someone," he said. "What are you doing here?"

From behind him, Clark heard Señora Lily say, "Speak right up, Mr. Lewis."

"Please don't sell her!" Clark cried. "Please don't sell Carrie."

Chapter Seven

Clark Makes a Plea

Mr. Kramer stared at the sky and sucked in his breath. He pursed his lips and blew the air back out. Clark knew how much effort it was taking for Mr. Kramer not to yell at him. The urge to turn and run was strong, but Clark swallowed hard and stood his ground.

"Good morning, Señora Lily," Mr. Kramer said, ignoring Clark's plea. "Why aren't you at the parade like you're supposed to be?"

The man in the white hat had black eyes and long, shiny black hair. A leather string tied his hair at the back of his neck. Although his face showed no expression, Clark knew the man was watching him intently. Once his gaze strayed to Señora Lily, but it quickly returned to Clark.

"Good morning, Mr. Kramer," said Señora Lily. "I do believe Mr. Lewis has a mission to accomplish today. One that he believes is greater than riding in a parade."

"I know I'm making you really mad," Clark said to Mr. Kramer, "but could you just put off selling the cow until her calf is a little older?"

"The deal is final," Mr. Kramer said, with his eyes fixed on Clark. "We were signing the papers when you disturbed us."

Clark thought Mr. Kramer's eyes were like two hard, cold pieces of ice.

There was the rustle of silk as Señora Lily held her skirt a few inches off the ground and stepped closer to the porch.

"Mr. Kramer, we have not had the pleasure of meeting your friend," Señora Lily said.

Mr. Kramer pressed his lips together and shook his head. Again, he breathed in deeply and blew out a long stream of air before he spoke.

"Señora Lily, this is Mr. David Goodwater, a rancher from Montana," Mr. Kramer said. "Let's not keep him. He has a long trip home with that cow, and I have important business this morning."

Mr. Goodwater's spurs jingled as he came down the steps to shake hands with Señora Lily.

"How do you do?" she inquired.

"Glad to meet you," replied Mr. Goodwater. "Nice horses you've got."

Jamilla swished her tail and took a few steps toward Mr. Goodwater.

"Why yes," Señora Lily said. "The horses are truly a treasure. This is Mr. Clark Lewis. He's the reason I'm here," she continued. "By the way, those are mighty fine spurs you're wearing, Mr. Goodwater—just like mine."

Mr. Kramer glanced at his watch and was about to say something when Señora Lily lifted her long silk skirt and shook one black-booted foot. Her spurs made lovely music. She tipped back her head and laughed. A rosebud dangled over her ear. She pulled it out and stood with it in her hand.

Mr. Goodwater's lips didn't smile, but his eyes did. Mr. Kramer's eyes, on the other hand, had a way of frowning.

An idea came to Clark that made his knees feel shaky. He hoped he wouldn't have to herd the animals into Mr. Kramer's yard to protest. Instead, maybe Mr. Goodwater could help him! He was a kind man, so he might understand why Carrie shouldn't be separated from her baby. That would solve the whole problem.

Clark moistened his lips and took a step closer to Mr. Goodwater.

"I know this will come as a big surprise to you," Clark said, looking up at Mr. Goodwater, "but that horse right there can talk."

"Oh me! Oh my!" Mr. Kramer shouted. "Why are you telling him that ridiculous story?"

Mr. Goodwater seemed not to hear Mr. Kramer. He just kept watching Clark calmly. For a moment it seemed like Mr. Goodwater's expression changed ever so slightly. It was as though a tiny light went on in his black eyes. Clark decided he liked Mr. Goodwater's eyes.

"I came here yesterday to see the horse I'd ride in the parade, and that horse talked to me," Clark said, pointing to Jamilla. "She said the cow you're buying has a calf who hasn't eaten for days because she's so sad over her mother being taken away. She's starving, and now her mother won't eat, either," Clark continued. "We don't want you to buy the cow and take her from her calf. Please, sir."

"He's already bought and paid for the cow!" Mr. Kramer shouted. "Can't you understand that?"

There was silence, and Clark's heart felt cold. Even the horses stood still. The scent of Señora Lily's rosebud bouquet hung in the warm air.

The awful moment was broken by crunching gravel as Mr. Goodwater squatted down and placed one hand on the ground for balance. Now Clark didn't have to stare up at the man, and he was relieved that Mr. Goodwater wasn't laughing. Instead, it seemed like he was waiting for the story to continue.

"Dave, let's get this done with because . . ." Mr. Kramer didn't finish what he was saying. Mr. Goodwater held up one hand as though to say he was taking a moment to listen to Clark.

Clark started talking as fast as he could because there was so much to tell.

"The President of the United States is here today," Clark began breathlessly, "and I won the essay contest. I was going to meet the President because of that. Then Señora Lily and I had to ride out here at the last minute and ask you not to buy the cow. We didn't think you'd come until tomorrow," Clark said, taking a breath. "We were surprised when we heard you were here. We were scared. We weren't late because Jamilla can make time stop. All these shiny things fall out of her hair when she does it, and it makes the air look sparkly. I guess you're surprised to hear that too, huh?"

It was a moment before Mr. Goodwater took his eyes off Clark and stood up. Clark wished the man would say something. He wanted to know what Mr. Goodwater thought about the fantastic story he just told him.

"You spoke your piece just fine," Señora Lily said. "I couldn't have done it better myself."

Jamilla whinnied and Mr. Goodwater walked back up onto the porch, his spurs jingling. He had neither smiled nor frowned. Clark took another breath. Why didn't Mr. Goodwater say something?

"Dave, we have to get a move on if we're going to get that cow," Mr. Kramer said.

There was a tight feeling in Clark's throat as Mr. Goodwater turned to go inside.

"You're still going to take the cow, aren't you?" Clark cried in a voice that was hoarse and thick.

"Yup," Mr. Goodwater said.

The tightness in Clark's throat became a lump. He swallowed hard and rubbed his neck to make the lumpy feeling go away. He'd made a fool of himself. Who would believe the story he'd just told? No wonder Willy teased him.

"I sure am sorry you got held up like this," Mr. Kramer said, as he held the screen door open for his guest. Mr. Goodwater stopped at the door and turned to Clark and Señora Lily.

"Nice meeting you all," he said, before disappearing inside the ranch house.

Mr. Kramer paused to look back at Clark. "Guess your plan didn't work. Business is business. Don't worry, son. You'll learn."

Everything was becoming a bit blurred by the warm tears welling up in Clark's eyes.

"All is not lost yet," Jamilla said, as she gave Clark a gentle nudge with her nose. "Are you ready with that backup plan?"

Señora Lily stepped back toward Jamilla and tucked a rosebud in her horse's harness.

"What can I do to help?" Señora Lily asked.

The day had grown warm, but the ocean breeze blew through the elm trees and cooled Clark's face. It helped soothe his feelings, too, while his friend's kind words helped the ache in his throat.

Clark brushed at a tear on his cheek and wondered if Señora Lily would try to stop his

backup plan. If she didn't, maybe she would help herd animals onto Mr. Kramer's driveway.

Mr. Goodwater and Mr. Kramer came back out of the house. Once again, the Montana man nodded to Señora Lily and Clark. Mr. Kramer ignored them both and hopped in the cattle truck with Mr. Goodwater. They followed the road that led to the corral.

It was useless for Clark to try to stretch his neck and see what was going on. Elm trees blocked much of his view of the barn and stables. Besides, the front of the buildings didn't face the ranch house.

The rumble of the truck engine stopped. Cowhands shouted and truck doors slammed. Then came a sound that made Clark's heart drop down to the ground. Rosebud was bawling! Even worse, Carrie had started mooing, too.

"She's going!" Jamilla exclaimed. "My dear friend Carrie is on her way out!"

Chapter Eight

Clark Gets the Surprise of His Life

"Señora Lily, we have to mount up!" Clark cried. "We have to herd the animals onto the driveway."

"Whatever for?" Señora Lily asked, climbing into her saddle and adjusting her red silk skirt around it.

"To peacefully protest," Clark said. "It's part of what people sometimes do to be heard."

Señora Lily stopped fixing her skirt. She raised her eyebrows at Clark and whistled sharply.

"A peaceful protest!" she cried. "Now that's an idea! What made you think of it?"

"I read about one in the paper," Clark said. "The animals will block the driveway to help us protest the sale of Carrie. Mr. Goodwater will get tired of waiting for them to move and maybe decide not to buy Carrie after all. The animals are going to run from Mr. Kramer when he tries to load them into trucks for the rodeo. He'll get worried about being late."

Señora Lily smiled and said, "Oh, I understand. You think our gentlemen friends will be convinced they should leave the cow with her calf."

"I can't think of anything else to do," Clark said.

"It's worth a try, and Jamilla says people can do more than they think," Señora Lily agreed.

"That's true," Jamilla said. "If they only tried."

Clark and Señora Lily glanced toward the corral, where Rosebud's bawling had become louder.

"Poor little thing," Señora Lily said.

"No one gets hurt during a peaceful protest," Clark explained. "I read about some factory workers who protested, and their bosses finally listened to what they had to say. In the end, they got better wages to feed their families, and they all were friends again."

"So you think a peaceful protest will force Mr. Kramer to stop and really listen to what you have to say about Rosebud?" Señora Lily asked.

"That's my plan," Clark said. "We'll have one last chance to ask Mr. Kramer and Mr. Goodwater to listen to us."

"I can see you've put your whole heart into this," Señora Lily said, "so let's give it a try."

"The animals are ready to help," Jamilla said. "All I need to do is give the word. The geese are mischievous ones, though. You never know what they'll do."

At that very moment a few geese and chickens came strutting by, and Clark tried herding them toward the ranch house. The chickens dashed about in a circle, and the geese waddled off down the road.

"Jamilla, will you tell the animals what we need them to do?" Clark asked.

Several bay and chestnut horses were munching on scattered bales of hay in the corral. As Clark and Señora Lily rode into the enclosure, Jamilla tossed her head and whinnied. The animals stopped eating and perked up their ears. They whinnied back and trotted toward the palomino. Clark knew they must be answering Jamilla's call for assistance. Whistler responded to Clark's prodding as the horses pranced single file through the narrow gate.

"Yee-haw!" Clark shouted, as he rode behind the horses.

"Go on now!" Señora Lily called, as she herded them toward the ranch house.

The horses stirred up a cloud of dust as they clattered onto the road. The chickens squawked as they dashed about, but the geese stopped right in the middle of the road. Soon most of the horses were in front of Mr. Kramer's house. They snorted and shuffled about, but all seemed content to linger on the driveway.

"They'll stay put until I tell them to move," Jamilla called.

"That's amazing!" Clark exclaimed. "Jamilla, let's go get the mules in the next paddock."

There were only five mules in the paddock. A few swished flies with their tails, and one was rubbing the rail fence to scratch its itchy flanks. Señora Lily held Jamilla's reins as her horse trotted into the corral. The mules stopped their tail-swishing and flank-scratching when Jamilla whinnied. They clomped toward her with screeching, honking hee-haws that made Clark want to plug his ears.

Soon there was a fine collection of horses, mules, and chickens on Mr. Kramer's driveway. No one could travel down the road without chasing the animals back into their enclosures.

"There's something in the air," Señora Lily said, as she reined in Jamilla. "I feel a tickle in my bones."

Something had changed. Clark felt it, too. Rosebud was too quiet. He wished the calf would bawl just so he'd know Rosebud was still okay.

There was the grinding noise of a pickup truck's engine being started. Clark could hear it begin to chug along. It soon appeared on the road behind the ranch house.

It felt like someone had put a stone in Clark's stomach when he saw Mr. Kramer in the truck. This was it! What would the rancher do now?

Mr. Kramer brought his pickup to a halt near the animals. He rolled down his window and stuck his head out. His green eyes glared, and his mouth was set in a grim, straight line.

"What are you doing with those horses?" he yelled over the roar of the engine. "Clark, you better get them back in that paddock right now!"

Clark's mouth went dry, and he was speechless.

"Ease up on the boy, Mr. Kramer," Señora Lily said. "He means no harm. He feels like it's up to him to save the life of a little calf. He's in the mood for a little peaceful protest."

Clark found his voice and pleaded, "Please, sir, will you listen to me just one last time?"

"No, I will not!" Mr. Kramer shouted. "Are you trying to ruin my whole day? Put my horses back in the corral before David Goodwater drives his truck around here! If you only knew what I still had to do today. Ride fast and you'll still make it to the parade in town. It's not noon yet."

Then came a dreadful sight. The cattle truck had appeared on the road leading from the cattle pens. Carrie was inside, and she was leaving forever. Rosebud was doomed!

"Jamilla!" Clark cried. "Jamilla, stop time, please! I need to think."

"Yes, we do need a think session," Señora Lily added.

"It's worth one last try," the palomino said. "Defeat may be at hand, yet perhaps we can turn it into triumph. It may not be too late!"

Jamilla tossed her head and sent her bright golden mane twisting and flying about her head. Sprinkles of light flooded the air above Clark and Señora Lily.

"I'll never forget the first time I saw her do that," Señora Lily said, lifting her face toward the whirling shower of light.

Tiny tingles of coolness dotted Clark's face and hands as the bits of light settled on him. The Appaloosa breathed softly. Clark thought that if Whistler were a cat, he would have purred. In a few moments the twirling sparkles subsided.

Mr. Kramer sat in his pickup with his mouth open and a fixed scowl on his face. On the driveway, the horses' hooves were raised in midair. The locks on their manes were caught in a bouncing motion. It was funny to see their manes sticking out stiffly from their necks. The pickup's engine gave a monotonous, unchanging whine. The wings of the geese were stretched out stiffly, and one stray feather was caught in the air just above the ground.

Jamilla and Whistler stamped their feet nervously. Señora Lily sat watching Clark with a questioning look on her face.

What more could he do? Clark took his hat

from his head and wiped his brow. He'd begged Mr. Kramer to listen. He'd begged Mr. Goodwater to listen. He'd sacrificed his place in the parade. He'd tried to organize the animals in protest. Nothing had worked.

"The only thing I can do now is come here everyday and take care of Rosebud," Clark sighed. "Maybe if we give her lots of love and attention she'll eat again and survive."

"Of course we'll do that," Señora Lily said, adjusting herself to a more comfortable position in the saddle. "I'll be glad to help."

"You mustn't worry that you couldn't convince Mr. Goodwater to stop the sale of Carrie," Jamilla said. "I still think you're a very special young man, and you'll always be one of my truest friends."

"I feel exactly the same way," Señora Lily said.

For the second time that day Clark felt an awful, lumpy ache forming in his throat. Jamilla had said that when he'd failed with Mr. Kramer before. Tears welled up in Clark's eyes. He took a deep breath and rubbed his neck, hoping the tightness would go away. Señora Lily sat watching him, and her face seemed to soften.

Were her eyes watering, too? Clark wondered.

Clark did not want her to see him crying, so he looked toward the paddocks. That only reminded him that Rosebud was there all alone. Clark didn't want to think about that. Beyond the corrals was the black-topped highway. Clark focused his gaze there and tried to ignore the warm trickles that were running down his cheeks.

"I'm sorry for you, too, Jamilla," Clark said, in a choked voice. "You've lost your friend Carrie and . . ."

Something on the highway caught Clark's attention. He squinted his eyes and he sat up straighter in the saddle.

The geese on the road started honking and waddling around. The horses in the driveway began stirring restlessly. Then Mr. Goodwater's blue truck came rattling into view.

Mr. Kramer roared the pickup's engine as time resumed.

"You showed true character and courage in all this," Señora Lily said. "Why, you wouldn't give up at all. Even when it looked as though you surely couldn't win. I'm so proud of you I could . . ."

"Look!" Clark shouted, standing up in his stirrups. He was pointing toward the smooth, dark highway beyond. "Look at that!" he shouted once more.

Señora Lily looked, and her mouth dropped open.

"Well, as I live and breathe!" she cried.

From inside the pickup, Mr. Kramer was looking, too. He shoved his straw hat back on his head and gave a sharp cry of excitement. It startled the horses and made them dance. The cattle truck came to a halt, and Mr. Goodwater sat watching the main road with his hands on the steering wheel.

Down the highway sped two lines of motorcycle police. Squad cars followed with flashing red and blue lights. Two dark-colored vans traveled along after the police cars. Two helicopters flew just above the highway. Directly below the helicopters, a long, shiny black limousine zoomed along. It was flying the Stars and Stripes on both front fenders. Its doors had been polished so they gleamed like mirrors. On one of them, the seal of the President of the United States shone gloriously in the hot sun!

Chapter Nine

Clark's Plan Is Foiled

If Clark was shocked to see the President's entourage cruising down the highway, he was even more shocked at what happened in the next few seconds. The entire procession of vehicles turned onto the road that led to Mr. Kramer's ranch!

Jamilla and Whistler danced backward as the helicopters flew near. Señora Lily's red skirt rippled in the wind as she stood between the two horses. Mr. Kramer stuck his head out of the pickup window and began shouting at Clark.

"Move out of the way," he cried. "Move out of the way!"

Señora Lily took Jamilla's bridle and led her to the side of the road. She motioned for Clark to follow.

"The President is coming to the ranch!" Clark shouted, as he bounced up and down in the saddle.

"Of course he is," Mr. Kramer said. "Don't you think I know it? Now move your horse and the rest of these animals away from the driveway!"

Clark nudged the Appaloosa with his spurs and coaxed him to a place near Jamilla. Mr. Kramer parked his pickup under some trees near the ranch house. He jumped out of the vehicle and slammed the door as he scowled at Clark and Señora Lily.

"Mr. Kramer," Señora Lily cried, "why didn't you tell us the President was coming to your ranch?"

"Because it's no one's business except mine and the President's," Mr. Kramer said.

The rancher's green eyes were glittering, and his lips turned up in a half-smile. His expression was like Willy's the day he'd hidden Clark's lunch. Clark had looked for a long time before he found it.

"Besides," Mr. Kramer continued, "the Secret Service doesn't like people talking about where the President is going and when. They have to think about the President's security."

There was a terrible honking on the dirt road. The noise was not from the President's car, but from the two geese that had wandered there. The helicopters roared as they hovered over the President's limousine. Policemen sat with somber faces behind the wheels of their cars. A man in one of the vans talked into a cell phone as the entire motorcade came to a halt.

A door on one of the vans opened, and a man in dark glasses stepped out. He wore a dark suit with a small pin on the lapel. A short wire extended from his earphone to the inside of his shirt. His smooth hair was soon ruffled by the wind from the helicopters. He was not smiling.

It was a Secret Service agent! Clark's heart pounded with joy. He was seeing the President's personal bodyguards right up close.

The man shot an annoyed look at the geese, and frowned in the direction of the blue cattle truck. A motorcycle policeman climbed off his bike. He stood in the road, looking from the Secret Service agent to the geese, unsure of what to do.

The Secret Service agent motioned toward the blue truck. The motorcycle policeman

climbed back on his bike, sped to
Mr. Goodwater's truck, and skidded
around so he could look directly in the
truck's window. He kept pointing toward the
President's limousine as he spoke. The
policeman roared back to the motorcade, and
Mr. Goodwater moved his truck a short distance
off the dirt road.

"Someone get these geese off the road!" the
Secret Service agent shouted over the roar of the
helicopters' engines. "The President of the
United States would like to pass!"

Clark was off his horse in an instant. He ran

to the geese and tried to shoo them this way and that. To his surprise, they didn't scare easily. The policeman joined Clark and waved his arms at the geese. The helicopter blades beat the air and blew dust around. The wind from the blades pressed dimples into the feathers of the geese. The birds stood their ground, flapping their wings and honking. When Clark tried to shoo them a second time, they waddled toward him, not away from him!

"See what you've done," Mr. Kramer yelled. "I tried to get you out of here and back to the parade!"

"We had no idea the President was coming!" Señora Lily cried, holding onto the horses.

A door on the first van opened, and a lady in a dark pantsuit stepped out. She, too, had a pin on the lapel of her jacket and earphone wires hung alongside her neck. It looked like she was talking to her wrist, but Clark knew she must be speaking into a microphone. In a moment the helicopters flew away and touched down on one of Mr. Kramer's nearby fields. The dust on the road settled, and the roar of the helicopters quieted. Clark breathed a sigh of relief.

"Get some bread crumbs," the lady in the pantsuit said. "The geese will follow the food you offer."

The agent with the smooth hair shouted, "Move the horses and mules off the road first! The President has a schedule to keep."

Afterward, Clark didn't remember running to Whistler and mounting up again. But when it was all over, he had a fuzzy vision of himself herding horses, mules, and chickens back into their corrals. Señora Lily rode right beside him with her crimson skirt spread like a huge flower on Jamilla's back. In no time the animals were back in their enclosures.

"Ma'am!" Mr. Kramer called to the Secret Service agent. "Ma'am, I have the horses ready for the President to inspect. If you'll just drive around to the corral he can choose the one he wants to ride in the parade. My cowhands have orders to bring the stallions out the minute he arrives."

The President's motorcade started up again, and the limousine traveled slowly up the road to the ranch house and stopped. The lady in the pantsuit climbed back out of her van and spoke into the microphone at her wrist. Clark watched, mesmerized, as she walked toward Mr. Kramer.

"Bring the horses out here," she said. "We don't like the idea of driving around back. There are too many vehicles. The President will see the horses from his car."

"So the President is going to choose his horse for himself," Señora Lily said. "I've heard he's

83

mighty picky about the horse he rides."

"We haven't missed the parade if the President is here!" Clark exclaimed.

"We haven't saved Rosebud yet, either," Jamilla said.

A pang of guilt stung Clark's heart and made it beat rapidly for a moment. In all the excitement he'd forgotten about Rosebud!

Three cowhands were leading some prancing stallions from the stables. The horses walked one behind the other, making a mini-parade of their own. Mr. Kramer was led by the Secret Service agent to the window of the President's limousine. The cowhands arranged the horses in front of the President's car. Clark guessed the President must be choosing the horse he liked.

Mr. Kramer bent toward the window of the limousine and tipped his hat. Clark wondered if the President would notice that Mr. Kramer's eyes never smiled. Every so often Mr. Kramer said, "Yes sir," or "No sir," as he spoke to the Chief Executive.

Now another vehicle was coming down the gravel road from the stables. It was another pickup, and it was pulling a trailer for transporting horses.

Mr. Kramer moved back from the window of the limousine and shouted to a cowhand.

"Load up the white stallion, Abe!" Mr. Kramer yelled. "And make it snappy—the President is running late!"

The Secret Service agent jumped back in the van, and spoke into her wrist. The police cars and motorcycles began a short circular parade around Mr. Kramer's driveway so they could travel back toward the main highway. The helicopters lifted off the ground with a roar. Clark watched the sun gleam on the windows of the Presidential limousine as it moved down the gravel road.

"Now that was a once-in-a-lifetime sight!" Señora Lily exclaimed. "I've never herded horses for a President before!"

"I guess if my plans for a peaceful protest had to be ruined, I'd want them ruined by the President," Clark said. "At least that was a good reason."

"I had such strong, positive feelings about Mr. Goodwater," Jamilla said. "I thought we'd surely convinced him not to buy Carrie."

"Me too," Señora Lily said.

"Look," Clark exclaimed. "Mr. Goodwater

is getting out of his truck. I wonder if he's excited about seeing the President of the United States!"

"I wonder if he'll reconsider taking Carrie away," Jamilla said.

Chapter Ten

Clark's
Special Gift

$\mathcal{T}$he man from Montana climbed down from his truck and surveyed the scene before him. As Mr. Goodwater walked toward Clark, his eyes sparkled with merriment.

"I wish my wife could have seen that," Mr. Goodwater said. "She'll make me tell her about it over and over."

Mr. Kramer was heading Clark's way shouting, "No point in going into that cow-saving business now!"

There was a funny sinking sensation in Clark's heart. He stared at the ground. "After all my work, I didn't save Carrie," Clark said.

"Yes, you did!" Mr. Goodwater said, as he came up to Clark. "Maybe I should say you saved the calf."

Clark looked up at Mr. Goodwater, squinting

in puzzlement at his words.

"Isn't Carrie in the truck?" Clark asked.

"She is," Mr. Goodwater said, "but she's not alone."

"You mean . . . ?" Clark didn't finish what he was saying. He jumped off his horse and ran toward the blue cattle truck.

Señora Lily led both horses as she followed Clark. "I have a lovely feeling way down deep in my heart!" she said.

Before Clark could peer through the wooden stakes on the truck bed, a calf bawled. Jamilla snorted and danced sideways.

"Rosebud!" Clark shouted.

Clark pressed his face close to the boards and peered in. There in the cool dimness he saw Carrie, and next to her in the shadows was Rosebud. She was munching alfalfa!

"Rosebud is with her mother!" Clark cried.

"I knew it!" Jamilla said. "I knew I was right about Mr. Goodwater."

The palomino struck the ground with her hoof and snorted. Señora Lily gave her horse's neck a hug.

"You bought them both!" Clark cried, beaming his biggest smile at Mr. Goodwater.

"You believed me, didn't you?" Clark asked.

Clark would never forget what happened next. Mr. Goodwater's mouth opened in a wide smile. A smile that made his black eyes seem to dance with delight.

"You surprised me with your story," Mr. Goodwater said, "so I decided to give you a little surprise of my own. What I didn't know is that we'd all be surprised by the President."

As Mr. Goodwater spoke these last words, he looked toward the highway. Clark followed his gaze and thought the helicopters, motorcycle policemen, and squad cars made a beautiful sight as they cruised along with the Presidential limousine.

"Thank you, Mr. Goodwater," Clark said. "You're the nicest man I ever met, and I like the way your eyes smile."

Jamilla whinnied and tossed her head.

"Well, I'm not complaining," Mr. Kramer said. "I made two sales today instead of one."

"If you ever run for President, I'm voting for you, Clark," Señora Lily declared.

"I will, too," Mr. Goodwater said. "He makes great speeches."

The gravel crunched as Mr. Kramer turned

on his heels and started toward the porch.

The nagging little worry that had tormented Clark since yesterday morning vanished. He smiled because of that and because of an important decision he'd made.

"You know what?" Clark asked. "I know for sure what I want to be someday. I think my special gift is working with animals, so I'm going to be a vet."

Clark beamed as Señora Lily and Mr. Goodwater murmured their approval. Jamilla nudged Clark gently with her nose.

Mr. Goodwater turned to the Appaloosa and scratched its neck. "Beautiful," he said, before turning to stroke Jamilla's mane. "Look at that sparkle!" he said. "You'd think that mane could catch the sunlight."

Señora Lily winked at Clark and said, "Yes, Mr. Goodwater, you really would. Now, Clark, what do you say we ride out to Mission Gate and lead that parade after all? We can take our shortcut and be there before the President!"

Clark hugged Jamilla's neck and whispered in her ear, "We saved Rosebud, and we didn't even miss the parade or the President! Willy's still going to see me, too."

Señora Lily climbed on Jamilla, and Clark hopped on the Appaloosa. Mr. Goodwater climbed in his truck and started it. The geese waddled along, honking. The whole procession moved down the gravel driveway. Mr. Kramer stood on his porch with his hands in his pockets.

"Oh, I almost forgot," Clark called, as he turned to look at the rancher. "Carrie says she's very sorry for that time she kicked you when the vet came."

Mr. Kramer didn't return Clark's wave. He just stood there with a surprised and puzzled look on his face.

"This has been just about the best day in my whole life," Clark said to Jamilla. "But I have one last thing to ask you."

"What's that?" Jamilla asked.

"Could you teach me that time-stopping trick?"

"It's not a trick," Jamilla said. "It's a gift. Those who have it can catch the sunlight in their hair."

"Go ahead and try," Señora Lily said to Clark. "A winner like you can do anything."

Clark chewed on his lip a second before saying, "I don't have golden hair like Jamilla's, so I probably can't catch the sunlight."

"You can do more than you think," Jamilla said. "Give your head a good shake."

Clark shook his head as hard as he could.

"Goodness!" Señora Lily shouted. "Oh, my goodness!"

There in the air above Clark's head was a smattering of sparkles. A strange thrill started in Clark's heart. It spread throughout his whole body.

"Jamilla!" he cried. "I think I did it!"

"You *did* do it!" she answered.

Once again, Clark gave his head a good shake. Bits of sparkling sunlight flew in the air and landed on his cheeks. The cool tingly sensation filled Clark with delight.

"Know what, Jamilla? I'm going to miss Rosebud and Carrie, but I guess as long as they're together, that's what really matters."

Jamilla nodded thoughtfully.

"Know what else, Jamilla?" Clark said. "I think I like my long face. It's like yours, and yours is wonderful."

"I think your heart is like Jamilla's, too," Señora Lily said, "and that is what's most important."